BRAVO, Livingstone Mouse!

Pamela Duncan Edwards

ILLUSTRATED BY
Henry Cole

SCHOLASTIC INC.
New York Toronto London Auckland Sydney
Mexico City New Delhi Hong Kong Buenos Aires

One night Livingstone Mouse put on his explorer hat and set off to investigate the Wild Wood.

As Livingstone ran into a clearing, he found a woodpecker and a beaver building a stage.

"It's for the dance performances by special artists," said the woodpecker proudly. "The show starts in an hour."

"If you hurry, you might catch the foxes rehearsing their fox-trot," said the beaver, pointing to the edge of the clearing.

"Great," said Livingstone. "Save me a seat for the show."

As Livingstone ran on, he heard the sound of quarreling.

"The foxes are panicking," explained a cicada. "It's only an hour before the curtain goes up, and they still can't get their fox-trot right."

As Livingstone watched, the foxes started shuffling through the grass, arguing loudly.

"You stepped on my paw again!"
"It's your own fault. I've told you a hundred times—you go backward! I go forward!"
"I'm sorry I ever said I'd be your partner!"

"Excuse me," said Livingstone. "You really make a
handsome couple, but I think your rhythm's off."

"I beg your pardon!" said one of the foxes. "How many
times have you danced the fox trot?"

"Never!" replied Livingstone.

"Exactly!" cried the fox. "Why should we listen to someone with no fox-trot experience? Go away!"

"Pay no attention," the cicada told Livingstone. "Foxes are very bad-mannered."

As Livingstone and the cicada wandered off, they came across a bored-looking bee.

"The twist—rehearsal thirty-two," he buzzed with a yawn.

Half a dozen snakes reared up from the ground, wriggling violently.

"We're tied up again!" wailed one.

"That's because you keep going left when you should go right!" shouted another.

"Get your tail out of my eye!" bellowed a third.

"Excuse me," said Livingstone. "I really like the way you wriggle, but I think your rhythm's off."

"I beg your pardon!" said one of the snakes. "We do NOT wriggle. We slither! Do you slither?"

"No," replied Livingstone. "I scurry."

"Exactly!" cried the snake. "Why should we waste time speaking to a creature that scurries? Go away!"

"I'm fed up with these stubborn snakes," cried the bee, and he flew off with Livingstone and the cicada.

"Stupid shoes!" cried a voice suddenly, and a centipede stumbled into view.

"He's supposed to perform the clog dance tonight," chirruped a grasshopper. "But he keeps tripping over his boots."

"Excuse me," said Livingstone to the centipede. "I really like your shoes, but I think your rhythm's off."

"I beg your pardon!" said the centipede. "How many feet do you have?"

"Four," said Livingstone.

"Exactly!" cried the centipede. "How can a creature with four feet give advice to someone with fifty feet? Go away!"

"Wait for me," cried the grasshopper. "I've had enough of this bad-tempered centipede. I'm coming with you."

On a patch of grass, eight frogs faced each other in a square.

"Bow to your corner!" croaked a large frog. "Let me see," he cried. "Do-si-do! Yes, that's it— do-si-do. Take your partner! No—don't. Bow to each other instead—I think! Wait a minute!"

"Ouch!" cried the frogs as they fell over each other.

"He's mixing them all up," chirped a katydid.

"He's a hopeless square dance caller," giggled a cricket.

"I get so confused!" wailed the large frog.

"Excuse me," said Livingstone. "You have a beautiful voice, but I think your rhythm's off."

"I beg your pardon!" said the frog. "Did you SQUEAK?"

"Yes," replied Livingstone.

"Exactly!" cried the frog. "How can a creature that squeaks know anything about croaking square dance instructions? Go away!"

"How rude," tutted the katydid.

"Come with me," said Livingstone to the cicada, the bee, the grasshopper, the cricket, and the katydid. "I have an idea."

The moon was high as the woodland creatures gathered in the clearing.

"Quiet, please!" called the woodpecker. "For our first performance, the foxes will dance the fox-trot."

The terrified foxes stood staring at each other, paws rooted to the stage.

Then into the clearing marched Livingstone Mouse and His Insect Band, humming, buzzing, chirruping, chirping, and strumming. *Slow! Slow! Quick! Quick!* went the rhythm.

Suddenly, the foxes began to dance. Around and around they whirled in time to the music.

"What perfect rhythm!" cried the woodpecker. "What a perfect fox-trot!"

Livingstone raised his baton once more.

The band played "The Twist" for the snakes.
The snakes slithered and twisted, hissing with glee.

Click, clack, click went fifty centipede feet as the band played a clog dance.

The frogs bowed and do-si-doed, and do-si-doed again.

"Swing your partner," cried the frog as he croaked
his square dance instructions in time to the music.

At last, as pale light shone through the treetops, Livingstone laid down his baton.

"Three cheers for Maestro Livingstone Mouse!" cried the woodland creatures. "You saved our show. Will you play for all our performances?"

"I will," said Livingstone.

And that's exactly what he did!

To my sister, Maureen, with love
—P.D.E.
And to my sister, Trish, with love
—Pokey

No part of this publication may be reproduced in whole or in part, or stored in a retrieval system,
or transmitted in any form or by any means, electronic, mechanical, photocopying, recording,
or otherwise, without written permission of the publisher. For information regarding permission,
write to Hyperion Books for Children, an imprint of Disney Children's Book Group, LLC,
114 Fifth Avenue, New York, New York 10011.

ISBN 0-439-45976-1

Text copyright © 2000 by Pamela Duncan Edwards.
Illustrations copyright © 2000 by Henry Cole.
All rights reserved.
Published by Scholastic Inc., 555 Broadway, New York, NY 10012,
by arrangement with Hyperion Books for Children, an imprint of Disney Children's Book Group, LLC.
SCHOLASTIC and associated logos are trademarks and/or registered trademarks of Scholastic Inc.

12 11 10 9 8 7 6 5 4 3 2 1   2 3 4 5 6/0

Printed in the U.S.A.   14

First Scholastic printing, September 2001

The text is set in 20-pt. Packard Bold.
The artwork for each picture was prepared using acrylic paints and watercolor pencil
on hot press watercolor paper.
Designed by Christine Kettner